Tragedy of

Forbidden Love

Gary Austine Manuel

COPYRIGHT

DISCLAIMER

This is a fictional work. The characters, names, events, and settings represented in this story are completely the author's creation, and any resemblance to real individuals, living or dead, or actual events or settings is totally coincidental.

Table of Content

DEDICATION

I dedicate this story to my mother, Mrs. Beatrice Nwobu, who told me my first stories and kindled the love of storytelling in me. From the earliest days of my childhood, she filled my life with wonder and magic, and she taught me the power of the written word.

Thank you, Mom, for your love and support, and for instilling in me a love of literature and the arts. You are my inspiration, and I am forever grateful for the gifts you have given me. This story is for you, with all my love and gratitude.

ACKNOWLEDGEMENT

I would like to express my gratitude to the many people who have supported and encouraged me throughout the writing of this story.

Huge gratitude to Mrs. Beatrice Nwobu, who has always believed in me and encouraged me to follow my dreams. Your love and support means the world to me, and I am forever grateful for all that you have done for me.

I would also like to thank my friends and family, who have always been there for me, offering their love and support. You have been my rock through the good times and the bad, and I am forever grateful for your presence in my life.

Finally, I would like to thank the many authors and storytellers who have inspired me throughout the years. Your words have touched my heart and opened my mind, and I am forever grateful for the wisdom and insight you have shared with me. Thank you for helping to shape the person I am today.

About The Author

Gary Austine Manuel Ebuka Ugboma Esq FICMC, ACIArb UK, FMA, AGIS, PMP

LLB Hons, BA Hons, Dip Mus Ed, Pdip Bus Admin, PDip Estate Mgt, MBA, MSC Peace and conflict resolution.

Ebuka Ugboma has multiple degrees from different Universities across different fields; Arts, Law, Social Sciences and Humanities generally. He is a Chartered Arbitrator and Mediator, trained in the style and pattern of Chartered Institute Of Arbitrators UK.

Ebuka Ugboma has successfully published many books including Propensities And Habits For Success

Check out his books on Amazon:

https://www.amazon.com/Ebuka-Ugboma/e/B0B6HHVVW6

Email: info@affiliate-marketing.com.ng

Phone: +2348033924157

Chapter 1:

Introduction to Peter and Susan

INTRODUCTION

Meet Peter and Susan, the main characters of our story. Peter is the son of a fisherman, while Susan is the daughter of a wealthy merchant. Despite their differences in social status, these two young people fall deeply in love with each other. However, their families do not approve of their relationship, causing heartache and tragedy for the couple. Follow their love story as they navigate the challenges of their different family backgrounds and try to find happiness together.

Peter is a young man from a small village by the sea, where he lives with his father, a fisherman, and his mother. He is kind, hardworking, and deeply in love with Susan. Susan, on the other hand, is the daughter of a wealthy merchant who lives in the same village. She is intelligent, beautiful, and fiercely independent.

Despite their different social backgrounds, Peter and Susan are drawn to each other and fall deeply in love.

However, their love is not without its challenges. Peter's father believes that Susan is too high-born for his son, while Susan's mother sees Peter as nothing more than a poor fisherman's son. Despite their attempts to keep their relationship hidden, eventually their families find out about their love, and they forbid the couple from seeing each other again. Heartbroken, Peter is forced to leave the village to find work elsewhere, while Susan is left behind to mourn the loss of her beloved.

Follow their story as they try to navigate the challenges of their different family backgrounds and find happiness together. Will their love be strong enough to overcome the barriers that stand in their way? Read on to find out.

Our story takes place in a small village by the sea, where the air is filled with the salty scent of the ocean and the sound of waves crashing against the shore. The village is a bustling place, with narrow cobblestone streets and colorful houses dotting the landscape.

Peter and Susan both call this village home. Peter's family lives in a small cottage by the harbor, where his father works as a fisherman, setting out to sea each morning in his boat. Susan's family lives in a grand mansion on the outskirts of the village, where her father runs a successful merchant business. Despite their different circumstances, Peter and Susan both love the village and the close-knit community that resides there. It is in this idyllic setting that their love story begins.

The small village by the sea is a charming place, nestled along the coast of a picturesque bay. It is a bustling hub of activity, with fishermen setting out to sea each morning, merchants selling their wares at the market, and villagers going about their daily lives. The streets are narrow and winding, with cobblestone pathways and colorful houses lining the way.

Peter's family lives in a small cottage by the harbor, where they have lived for generations. The cottage is modest, with a thatched roof and a cozy interior. Peter's father, a rugged and weathered man, has spent most of his life at sea, braving the elements to bring in a catch for his family and the village. Peter helps his father with the fishing when he is not attending school, learning the ropes of the trade and dreaming of the day when he will take over the family business.

Susan's family, on the other hand, lives in a grand mansion on the outskirts of the village. The mansion is a grand and stately structure, with marble columns and a sprawling garden. Susan's father is a successful merchant, trading in exotic goods from distant lands. Susan has been raised in luxury, with all the comforts and privileges that come with her family's wealth. Despite her privileged upbringing, Susan is a kind and compassionate young woman, who cares deeply for those less fortunate than her.

It is in this idyllic village by the sea that Peter and Susan's love story begins. Despite their differences in social status, they are drawn to each other and fall deeply in love. However, as they soon discover, their love is not without its challenges, as they must navigate the obstacles of their different family backgrounds. Will their love be strong enough to overcome these barriers? Read on to find out.

Chapter 2:

The Meeting

Peter and Susan first meet on a bright and sunny afternoon at the market, where Susan is shopping with her mother. Peter is there with his father, selling their catch of the day at their usual stall. As Susan wanders through the crowded market, her eyes are drawn to Peter, who is standing behind his stall, chatting with a customer. He is tall and handsome, with a kind and friendly face. Susan can't help but feel drawn to him, and finds herself lingering near his stall to listen to his stories about life at sea.

Peter, too, is smitten with Susan from the moment he sees her. She is beautiful and intelligent, with a sparkle in her eyes and a quick wit. He can't help but be drawn to her, and starts to find excuses to linger near her, striking up conversations and offering to carry her packages.

As they spend more time together, their attraction deepens, and they begin to spend every moment they can together. They go for walks along the beach, watching the sunset and sharing their hopes and dreams for the future. They dance in the moonlight, lost in each other's embrace. Despite the barriers that stand between them, their love flourishes, and they can't imagine a life without each other.

As their relationship grows, Peter and Susan become inseparable, spending every moment they can together. They walk hand in hand along the beach, watching the sunset and dreaming of their future. They dance in the moonlight, lost in each other's embrace. Despite the challenges that stand between them, their love is strong, and they are determined to make a life together.

Peter and Susan's initial attraction to each other is instantaneous and electric. From the moment they lay eyes on each other, they feel an intense pull towards one another, as if they have known each other for a lifetime. They are drawn to each other's kind and friendly personalities, and find themselves lingering near each other, eager to spend more time together.

As they spend more time together, their attraction deepens, and they begin to develop strong feelings for each other. They share stories about their lives and their dreams, and find that they have a deep connection and understanding of one another. They enjoy each other's company and look forward to their time together, and it is clear to both of them that this is more than just a passing infatuation.

As their feelings for each other grow, they become more and more enamored with each other, and it is clear to them that this is the start of something special. They are head over heels in love, and can't imagine a life without each other. Despite the challenges that stand between them, they are determined to make their love work, and to find a way to be together forever.

Chapter 3:

Falling in Love

As Peter and Susan spend more time together, their love for each other deepens and grows stronger. They are drawn to each other's kindness, intelligence, and sense of humor, and find that they have a deep connection and understanding of one another. They share their hopes, dreams, and deepest secrets, and find solace in each other's embrace.

They spend every moment they can together, going on long walks along the beach, watching the sunset, and dancing in the moonlight. They are happy and content in each other's company, and it is clear to them that this is the start of something special.

Despite the challenges that stand between them, their love for each other is unwavering. They are determined to make their love work, and to find a way to be together forever. They dream of a future together, where they can live and love without the barriers of their different family backgrounds.

As their love grows, they become more and more enamored with each other, and it is clear to them that this is the real deal. They are head over heels in love, and can't imagine a life without each other. They are each other's rock, and their love gives them the strength and courage to face whatever challenges come their way.

As they grow closer and more in love, they begin to make plans for their future together. They dream of starting a family and building a home by the sea, where they can live and love without the constraints of their different family backgrounds. They know that their love will be tested, but they are confident in their ability to weather any storm, as long as they have each other.

Despite the challenges that stand between them, Peter and Susan's love for each other remains strong and true. They are committed to making their love work, and to finding a way to be together forever. They know that their love is worth fighting for, and they are determined to make their dreams a reality. So, they hold on to each other and their love with all their might, and they are confident that they will overcome any obstacle that comes their way.

Peter and Susan's love for each other is deep and true, and they are happiest when they are together. They spend every moment they can together, going on long walks along the beach, watching the sunset, and dancing in the moonlight. These are the moments that they cherish the most, when they can be alone and lost in each other's embrace, without the constraints of their different family backgrounds.

As they walk along the beach, they hold hands and share their dreams and hopes for the future. They watch the sunset and marvel at the beauty of the world around them. They talk about their plans for their future together, and imagine all the adventures they will have.

When they dance in the moonlight, they feel as if they are floating on air, lost in each other's embrace. They move effortlessly to the music, lost in their own little world. They are happy and content in each other's company, and it is clear to them that this is the start of something special.

Despite the challenges that stand between them, their love for each other is unwavering. They are determined to make their love work, and to find a way to be together forever. They know that their love is worth fighting for, and they are confident in their ability to weather any storm, as long as they have each other.

So, they hold on to each other and their love with all their might, and they are confident that they will overcome any obstacle that comes their way. They are happy and content in each other's company, and they look forward to all the adventures and happiness that their future together will bring. Their love for each other is a bright and shining beacon, lighting their way through even the darkest of times. They are grateful for every moment they have together, and they cherish the memories of their happy times together, knowing that they will always be a part of them.

Peter and Susan have big dreams and hopes for their future together. They dream of building a home by the sea, where they can live and love without the barriers of their different family backgrounds. They envision a life filled with laughter, adventure, and happiness, where they can be free to be themselves and follow their hearts.

They talk about starting a family, and raising children in their idyllic seaside home. They imagine spending their days exploring the world, traveling to distant lands, and experiencing all that life has to offer. They dream of growing old together, surrounded by the love and laughter of their family and friends.

They also hope to make a positive impact in the world, using their love and their talents to make a difference in the lives of others. They believe in the power of love to change the world, and they are determined to spread joy and hope wherever they go.

Despite the challenges that stand between them, Peter and Susan are confident in their ability to make their dreams a reality. They are determined to make their love work, and to find a way to be together forever. They know that their love is worth fighting for, and they are willing to do whatever it takes to make their dreams come true.

So, they hold on to each other and their love with all their might, and they are confident that they will overcome any obstacle that comes their way. They are excited for all the adventures and happiness that their future together will bring, and they can't wait to see what the future holds for them.

Chapter 4:

Family Opposition

Despite the deep love that Peter and Susan have for each other, their families do not approve of their relationship. Peter's father, a rugged fisherman, believes that Susan is too high-born for his son, and he forbids Peter from seeing her again. Susan's mother, a wealthy merchant, sees Peter as nothing more than a poor fisherman's son, and she is disgusted by their relationship.

The news of their families' disapproval comes as a crushing blow to Peter and Susan, who had hoped that their love would be accepted and supported. They are heartbroken at the thought of being separated, and they beg their families to reconsider their decision. However, their pleas fall on deaf ears, and they are left with no choice but to part ways.

Peter is forced to leave the village to find work elsewhere, while Susan is left behind to mourn the loss of her beloved. The separation is painful and difficult for both of them, and they struggle to come to terms with their families' decision.

As the years pass, Peter works hard to make a new life for himself, eventually becoming a successful merchant and marrying a woman from a neighboring village. However, he never forgets about Susan, and the love he has for her never dies.

Susan, on the other hand, remains in the village, working as a seamstress and dreaming of the day when Peter will return to her. She holds on to the memories of their happy times together, and she never stops hoping that they will find a way to be together again.

However, fate has other plans, and Susan falls ill with a fever that takes her life before Peter can ever come back to her. In the end, Peter and Susan's love is doomed to tragedy due to their different family backgrounds. But even in death, their love remains strong, and they are reunited in the great beyond, forever bound by the love they had shared in life.

Peter and Susan's families are opposed to their relationship for a variety of reasons, including social status and class differences. Peter's father, a rugged fisherman, believes that Susan is too high-born for his son, and he forbids Peter from seeing her again. He is concerned about the social and economic implications of their relationship, and he wants what is best for his son.

Susan's mother, a wealthy merchant, sees Peter as nothing more than a poor fisherman's son, and she is disgusted by their relationship. She is concerned about the social and economic implications of their relationship, and she wants what is best for her daughter. She believes that Susan can do better, and she wants her daughter to marry someone of her own social standing.

These class and social status differences are a major barrier between Peter and Susan, and they are a source of tension and conflict between their families. Despite their deep love for each other, they are unable to overcome these barriers, and they are forced to part ways.

The separation is painful and difficult for both of them, and they struggle to come to terms with their families' decision. They are heartbroken at the thought of being separated, and they beg their families to reconsider their decision. However, their pleas fall on deaf ears, and they are left with no choice but to part ways.

As the years pass, Peter and Susan struggle to move on from their love, but they are never able to forget about each other. They hold on to the memories of their happy times together, and they never stop hoping that they will find a way to be together again. However, fate has other plans, and their love is doomed to tragedy due to their different family backgrounds. Even in death, their love remains strong, and they are reunited in the great beyond, forever bound by the love they had shared in life.

As Peter and Susan's love for each other grows, they become increasingly aware of the barriers that stand between them, and they are forced to keep their love hidden from their families. They know that their families will never accept their relationship, and they are terrified at the thought of being separated.

They are careful to keep their love a secret, meeting in secret and speaking in hushed tones whenever they are together. They sneak away from their families to spend time alone, seeking out hidden corners and secluded beaches where they can be alone and free to express their love.

Despite their efforts to keep their love hidden, it is not long before their families find out about their relationship. Peter's father is furious, and Susan's mother is disgusted. They forbid the young couple from seeing each other again, and Peter is forced to leave the village to find work elsewhere.

The news of their families' disapproval comes as a crushing blow to Peter and Susan, who had hoped that their love would be accepted and supported. They are heartbroken at the thought of being separated, and they beg their families to reconsider their decision. However, their pleas fall on deaf ears, and they are left with no choice but to part ways.

As the years pass, Peter and Susan struggle to move on from their love, but they are never able to forget about each other. They hold on to the memories of their happy times together, and they never stop hoping that they will find a way to be together again. However, fate has other plans, and their love is doomed to tragedy due to their different family backgrounds. Even in death, their love remains strong, and they are reunited in the great beyond, forever bound by the love they had shared in life.

Chapter 5:

Separation

The moment when Peter and Susan's families find out about their relationship is a pivotal and emotional one, filled with tension and conflict. It is a turning point in their relationship, and it marks the beginning of the end for their love.

The discovery happens on a bright and sunny afternoon, as Peter and Susan are walking along the beach. They are deep in conversation, lost in their own little world, when they hear a voice calling their names. They turn to see Peter's father, a rugged fisherman, striding towards them with a stormy expression on his face.

Peter's father is livid, and he is furious with his son for falling in love with Susan. He sees Susan as being too high-born for his son, and he is concerned about the social and economic implications of their relationship. He forbids Peter from seeing Susan again, and he orders his son to leave the village to find work elsewhere.

Susan's mother, a wealthy merchant, is equally disgusted by their relationship. She sees Peter as nothing more than a poor fisherman's son, and she is concerned about the social and economic implications of their relationship. She wants what is best for her daughter, and she believes that Susan can do better. She forbids Susan from seeing Peter again, and she orders her daughter to stay away from him.

The news of their families' disapproval comes as a crushing blow to Peter and Susan, who had hoped that their love would be accepted and supported. They are heartbroken at the thought of being separated, and they beg their families to reconsider their decision. However, their pleas fall on deaf ears, and they are left with no choice but to part ways.

As the years pass, Peter and Susan struggle to move on from their love, but they are never able to forget about each other. They hold on to the memories of their happy times together, and they never stop hoping

When Peter's father and Susan's mother find out about their relationship, their reactions are strong and emotional. Peter's father is livid, and he is furious with his son for falling in love with Susan. He sees Susan as being too high-born for his son, and he is concerned about the social and economic implications of their relationship. He forbids Peter from seeing Susan again, and he orders his son to leave the village to find work elsewhere.

Susan's mother, a wealthy merchant, is equally disgusted by their relationship. She sees Peter as nothing more than a poor fisherman's son, and she is concerned about the social and economic implications of their relationship. She wants what is best for her daughter, and she believes that Susan can do better. She forbids Susan from seeing Peter again, and she orders her daughter to stay away from him.

Their forbidding of the couple from seeing each other again is a crushing blow to Peter and Susan, who had hoped that their love would be accepted and supported. They are heartbroken at the thought of being separated, and they beg their families to reconsider their decision. However, their pleas fall on deaf ears, and they are left with no choice but to part ways.

The separation is painful and difficult for both of them, and they struggle to come to terms with their families' decision. They are forced to say goodbye to each other, knowing that it may be the last time they ever see each other. Despite their deep love for each other, they are unable to overcome.

The separation of Peter and Susan is a heart-wrenching and painful event, filled with heartbreak and pain. They are devastated at the thought of being separated, and they beg their families to reconsider their decision. However, their pleas fall on deaf ears, and they are left with no choice but to part ways.

The separation is particularly difficult for Peter, who is forced to leave the village to find work elsewhere. He is torn between his love for Susan and his duty to his family, and he knows that he has no choice but to leave. He is heartbroken at the thought of leaving Susan behind, but he knows that it is the only way to honor his family's wishes.

As he packs his bags and prepares to leave, Peter can't help but feel a sense of despair. He knows that he is leaving behind the love of his life, and he can't imagine living his life without Susan by his side. He is filled with regret and sadness, and he can't help but wonder if things could have been different.

Despite his heartbreak, Peter is determined to make a new life for himself. He works hard to build a new career and to create a future for himself, but he never forgets about Susan. The love he has for her never dies, and he holds on to the hope that they will one day be reunited.

As for Susan, she remains in the village, working as a seamstress and dreaming of the day when Peter will return to her. She holds on to the memories of their happy times together, and she never stops hoping that they will find a way to be together again. However, fate has other plans, and their love is doomed to tragedy due to their different family backgrounds. Even in death, their love remains strong, and they are reunited in the great beyond, forever bound by the love they had shared in life.

Chapter 6:

Peter's New Life

After leaving the village to find work elsewhere, Peter works hard to make a new life for himself. He is determined to succeed, and he puts all of his effort into building a new career. He is a hard worker, and he quickly rises through the ranks, becoming a successful merchant in his own right.

As he builds his business, Peter never forgets about Susan. The love he has for her never dies, and he holds on to the hope that they will one day be reunited. He thinks about her often, and he remembers the happy times they shared together.

Despite his success, Peter is not happy. He misses Susan deeply, and he feels a sense of emptiness and loneliness without her by his side. He wishes that things had turned out differently, and he regrets the choices he has made.

As the years pass, Peter becomes more and more successful, but he is still not satisfied. He knows that something is missing from his life, and he can't shake the feeling that he is incomplete without Susan. He longs to be reunited with her, and he dreams of a future where they can be together again.

Eventually, Peter meets a woman from a neighboring village, and he falls in love with her. She is kind, beautiful, and loving, and she makes Peter happy. He marries her, and they build a life together, but he never forgets about Susan. The love he has for her remains strong, and he is forever bound to her by the love they had shared in life.

Peter's marriage to Alice, a woman from a neighboring village, is a difficult one, as he struggles to move on from Susan. Despite his deep love for Alice, he can't shake the feeling that he is incomplete without Susan. He misses her deeply, and he feels a sense of emptiness and loneliness without her by his side.

At first, Peter tries to push these feelings aside, hoping that he can be happy with Alice. He loves her deeply, and he is grateful for the joy and happiness she brings into his life. However, no matter how hard he tries, he can't seem to shake his feelings for Susan.

As the years pass, Peter's love for Susan only grows stronger. He thinks about her often, and he remembers the happy times they shared together. He wonders what might have been if things had turned out differently, and he regrets the choices he has made.

His struggle to move on from Susan causes tension and conflict in his marriage to Alice. She can sense that he is not fully present in their relationship, and she becomes frustrated and hurt by his distant behavior. She tries to support him, but she can't seem to reach him, and she begins to feel that she is competing with a ghost.

Despite these struggles, Peter and Alice's love for each other remains strong. They work hard to overcome their difficulties, and they are determined to make their marriage a success. They support each other through the good times and the bad, and they remain committed to building a life together.

In the end, Peter is able to find some measure of peace and happiness with Alice, but he never forgets about Susan. The love he has for her remains strong, and he is forever bound to her by the love they had shared in life.

Despite his best efforts, Peter is never able to fully move on from Susan and the love he had for her. He misses her deeply, and he thinks about her often. He remembers the happy times they shared together, and he regrets the choices he has made.

His love for Susan is a constant presence in his life, and it shapes his relationships and his decisions. He is never able to fully commit to his marriage with Alice, as he is always comparing her to Susan. He becomes distant and distracted, and he is unable to fully engage in their relationship.

Alice is understanding and patient, and she tries to support Peter through his struggles. However, she can sense that he is not fully present in their relationship, and she becomes frustrated and hurt by his distant behavior. She tries to reach out to him, but she can't seem to get through to him, and she begins to feel that she is competing with a ghost.

Despite these struggles, Peter and Alice's love for each other remains strong. They work hard to overcome their difficulties, and they are determined to make their marriage a success. They support each other through the good times and the bad, and they remain committed to building a life together.

In the end, Peter is able to find some measure of peace and happiness with Alice, but he never forgets about Susan. The love he has for her remains strong, and he is forever bound to her by the love they had shared in life. Even in death, their love remains strong, and they are reunited in the great beyond, forever bound by the love they had shared in life.

Chapter 7:

Susan's Loneliness

After Peter leaves the village to find work elsewhere, Susan is left behind, heartbroken and alone. She is devastated at the thought of being separated from her true love, and she struggles to come to terms with her families' decision.

Despite her heartbreak, Susan tries to carry on with her life. She works as a seamstress, spending long hours at her sewing machine, trying to keep her mind occupied. She is a skilled seamstress, and she is well-respected in the village.

However, despite her success, Susan is not happy. She misses Peter deeply, and she feels a sense of emptiness and loneliness without him by her side. She holds on to the memories of their happy times together, and she never stops hoping that he will return to her.

As the years pass, Susan's love for Peter only grows stronger. She dreams of the day when he will return to her, and she holds on to the hope that they will one day be reunited. She writes letters to him, pouring her heart and soul into each one, hoping that they will find their way to him.

Despite her love for Peter, Susan's life is not easy. She is plagued by illness and hardship, and she is forced to face many challenges alone. She is strong, however, and she persists, holding on to the hope that she will one day be reunited with her beloved.

In the end, Susan's love for Peter is doomed to tragedy due to their different family backgrounds. She falls ill with a fever that takes her life before Peter can ever come back to her. Even in death, their love remains strong, and they are reunited in the great beyond, forever bound by the love they had shared in life.

After Peter leaves the village to find work elsewhere, Susan is left behind, heartbroken and alone. She is devastated at the thought of being separated from her true love, and she struggles to come to terms with her families' decision.

Despite her heartbreak, Susan tries to carry on with her life. She works as a seamstress, spending long hours at her sewing machine, trying to keep her mind occupied. However, despite her success, Susan is not happy. She misses Peter deeply, and she feels a sense of loneliness and longing without him by her side.

Susan is plagued by feelings of loneliness and longing for Peter. She thinks about him often, and she remembers the happy times they shared together. She holds on to the memories of their walks along the beach, their dances in the moonlight, and their shared dreams and hopes for the future. These memories sustain her, and they help her to hold on to the hope that they will one day be reunited.

Despite her love for Peter, Susan's life is not easy. She is plagued by illness and hardship, and she is forced to face many challenges alone. She is strong, however, and she persists, holding on to the hope that she will one day be reunited with her beloved.

In the end, Susan's love for Peter is doomed to tragedy due to their different family backgrounds. She falls ill with a fever that takes her life before Peter can ever come back to her. Even in death, their love remains strong, and they are reunited in the great beyond, forever bound by the love they had shared in life.

Chapter 8:

Peter's Memories of Susan

As the years pass, Peter never forgets about Susan and the love they shared. He thinks about her often, and he remembers the happy times they spent together. He remembers their walks along the beach, their dances in the moonlight, and their shared dreams and hopes for the future.

These memories are a constant presence in his life, and they shape his relationships and his decisions. He is never able to fully move on from Susan, and he is haunted by the thought of what might have been if things had turned out differently.

Peter's love for Susan is a constant source of pain and regret, and he is filled with sorrow at the thought of never being able to be with her again. He wonders what became of her, and he imagines her living a happy life in the village, surrounded by loved ones.

Despite his heartbreak, Peter is determined to make the best of his life. He works hard to build a successful career and to create a future for himself. He meets a woman from a neighboring village, Alice, and he falls in love with her. She is kind, beautiful, and loving, and she makes Peter happy.

However, despite his deep love for Alice, Peter can't shake the feeling that he is incomplete without Susan. He misses her deeply, and he feels a sense of emptiness and loneliness without her by his side. He becomes distant and distracted, and he is unable to fully engage in his relationship with Alice.

Despite these struggles, Peter and Alice's love for each other remains strong. They work hard to overcome their difficulties, and they are determined to make their marriage a success. They support each other through the good times and the bad, and they remain committed to building a life together.

In the end, Peter is able to find some measure of peace and happiness with Alice, but he never forgets about Susan. The love he has for her remains strong, and he is forever bound to her by the love they had shared in life. Even in death, their love remains strong, and they are reunited in the great beyond, forever bound by the love they had shared in life.

Throughout his life, Peter is plagued by regrets and a longing to be reunited with Susan. He misses her deeply, and he is filled with sorrow at the thought of never being able to be with her again. He wonders what became of her, and he imagines her living a happy life in the village, surrounded by loved ones.

His love for Susan is a constant source of pain and regret, and he is haunted by the thought of what might have been if things had turned out differently. He wonders if he made the right decision in leaving the village to find work elsewhere, and he regrets not fighting harder for his love for Susan.

Despite his best efforts, Peter is never able to fully move on from Susan and the love they shared. He becomes distant and distracted in his relationship with Alice, and he is unable to fully engage in their relationship. He is filled with guilt and remorse, and he wishes that he could turn back time and make things right.

Despite these struggles, Peter and Alice's love for each other remains strong. They work hard to overcome their difficulties, and they are determined to make their marriage a success. They support each other through the good times and the bad, and they remain committed to building a life together.

In the end, Peter is able to find some measure of peace and happiness with Alice, but he never forgets about Susan. The love he has for her remains strong, and he is forever bound to her by the love they had shared in life. Even in death, their love remains strong, and they are reunited in the great beyond, forever bound by the love they had shared in life.

Chapter 9:

Susan's Illness

As the years pass, Susan remains in the village, working as a seamstress and dreaming of Peter's return. Despite her heartbreak, she persists, holding on to the hope that they will one day be reunited. She writes letters to him, pouring her heart and soul into each one, hoping that they will find their way to him.

However, despite her love for Peter, Susan's life is not easy. She is plagued by illness and hardship, and she is forced to face many challenges alone. She is strong, however, and she persists, holding on to the hope that she will one day be reunited with her beloved.

One day, Susan falls ill with a fever that takes hold of her body and saps her strength. She becomes weak and tired, and she struggles to carry out her daily tasks. She is bedridden for weeks, unable to leave her bed.

As she lies in bed, Susan's health begins to decline. She becomes thin and pale, and her once bright eyes grow dull and lifeless. Despite her best efforts, she is unable to shake the fever, and it seems to be consuming her.

Her family and friends are worried, and they do everything they can to help her. They bring her food and drink, and they sit with her, offering her comfort and support. Despite their efforts, however, Susan's health continues to deteriorate.

In the end, Susan's love for Peter is doomed to tragedy due to their different family backgrounds. She falls ill with a fever that takes her life before Peter can ever come back to her. Even in death, their love remains strong, and they are reunited in the great beyond, forever bound by the love they had shared in life.

As Susan's health declines, she is faced with the reality of her impending death. She knows that she does not have much time left, and she begins to reflect on her life and the choices she has made.

She thinks about Peter, and she remembers the happy times they shared together. She remembers their walks along the beach, their dances in the moonlight, and their shared dreams and hopes for the future. She regrets the choices she has made, and she wishes that she could turn back time and make things right.

Despite her heartbreak, Susan is at peace with her fate. She knows that she has lived a good life, and she is grateful for the love and support of her family and friends. She says goodbye to them, telling them how much she loves them, and how much they mean to her.

As she lies in bed, waiting for the end, Susan is filled with a sense of longing and regret. She wishes that she could have one more chance to see Peter, and to tell him how much she loves him. She wonders if he is thinking of her, and if he is missing her as much as she is missing him.

In the end, Susan's love for Peter is doomed to tragedy due to their different family backgrounds. She falls ill with a fever that takes her life before Peter can ever come back to her. Even in death, their love remains strong, and they are reunited in the great beyond, forever bound by the love they had shared in life.

52

Chapter 10:

Peter's Return

After many years, Peter decides to return to the village where he and Susan had fallen in love. He is filled with a sense of longing and regret, and he is determined to see Susan one last time.

He packs his bags and sets out on the long journey back to the village. He travels over land and sea, through mountains and valleys, determined to reach his destination. The journey is long and difficult, but Peter is driven by his love for Susan, and he refuses to give up.

As he travels, Peter thinks about Susan and the love they shared. He remembers the happy times they spent together, and he regrets the choices he has made. He wonders if she is still alive, and if she is thinking of him. He hopes that she is happy, and that she has found love and happiness in her life.

Finally, after many weeks of travel, Peter arrives in the village. He is tired and worn, but he is filled with a sense of hope and excitement. He makes his way to Susan's house, his heart racing with anticipation.

As he approaches the house, he is filled with a sense of dread. He doesn't know what he will find, and he is afraid that he is too late. He knocks on the door, and he waits anxiously for an answer.

After what seems like an eternity, the door opens, and Peter is confronted by Susan's mother.

Chapter 11: Susan's Death

As Peter approaches Susan's bedside, he is filled with a sense of dread. He doesn't know what he will find, and he is afraid that he is too late. He approaches her cautiously, and he is shocked by what he sees.

Susan is lying in bed, her once vibrant and beautiful face now pale and gaunt. She is weak and tired, and she is barely able to lift her head. Her eyes are closed, and her breathing is shallow and labored.

Peter is filled with grief and sorrow at the sight of Susan in such a state. He falls to his knees by her bedside, and he takes her hand in his. He is filled with a sense of desperation and despair, and he is overwhelmed with emotion.

As he holds Susan's hand, Peter realizes that she is dying. He is filled with a sense of hopelessness and regret, and he is unable to hold back his tears. He remembers all the happy times they shared together, and he is filled with a sense of longing and regret.

Despite his pain, Peter is determined to be with Susan in her final moments. He stays by her side, holding her hand and talking to her softly. He tells her how much he loves her, and how much he regrets not being able to be with her.

In the end, Peter's love for Susan is doomed to tragedy due to their different family backgrounds. He arrives at her bedside too late, and he is unable to prevent her death. Even in death, their love remains strong, and they are reunited in the great beyond, forever bound by the love they had shared in life.